Tim's First Soccer Game

by

Susan O'Hara

Illustrated by Rebecca Barrett

Strategic Book Publishing and Rights Co.

Strategic Book Publishing and Rights Co.
12620 FM 1960, Suite A4-507
Houston, TX 77065
www.sbpra.com

ISBN: 978-1-61897-199-9

You made it easy to be your mom Bud!

"Cock-a-doodle-doo!" said the Nickelodeon alarm clock. "Cock-a-doodle-doo!"

Tim opened his eyes, looked at the purple Nickelodeon clock on his night stand. 7:00! It was time to get up, get dressed, and get to the game. He smiled and then jumped out of bed!

Soccer! How he loved the game! He loved to run. He loved to kick the ball. He loved to score!!

It all started when Tim's next door neighbor, Chris, gave Tim a soccer ball for a birthday gift.

Chris was in high school and was a really good soccer player. He showed Tim how to kick the ball and control it with his feet. Chris was really good at kicking the ball over and over again into the air with his foot.

He asked if Tim wanted to come see him play at his high school soccer game. "I'll try to score a goal for you, Tim," said Chris. Tim was so excited! He had never seen a soccer game before.

Tim, his sister Christie, Mom and Dad went to the game together. Chris was on the field with his team warming up when they arrived at the game. Chris turned and waved to Tim before the game started. Both teams moved into their positions on the field before the whistle blew. The ball went back and forth to the players on the field. It was passed to Chris who dribbled the ball up the field.

He went past the opposing player and passed it to a teammate. The teammate passed it back to Chris and he kicked it at the goal. Score! Chris pumped his fist into the air while his teammates gathered around to congratulate him on his goal. He yelled, "That was for you, Tim!"

When the announcement came to sign up for soccer, Tim, Christie, and Mom went to sign him up to be part of a team! Tim was the first one in line.

Then he went to a practice to meet the coach and the other players on the team. His team was named the Revolution! His shirt and socks were blue. It was Tim's favorite color. Coach Steve had passed out the team shirts, socks and shorts and talked to the players about the game of soccer. "Soccer is a lot of fun, but it can be hard work," said Coach Steve. "You need to try your hardest to be a good team player. Keep practicing when you go home. Try kicking the ball and practice scoring goals."

At practice, Coach Steve lined up all the kids on the field. When he blew the whistle to play, all the kids ran toward the ball to kick it toward their goal. Tim got there first and kicked the ball ahead of him. He passed it to his teammate, Ben.

21

Ben ran to the ball and passed it back to Tim. Tim kicked it at the goal. Score!!!! The team cheered with excitement! They continued to practice until the coach blew the whistle to stop. "Great practice kids! I'll see you here on Saturday for our first game," said Coach Steve.

So, today was the first game! Tim arrived at the field and joined the rest of the team to warm up. Coach Steve gathered everyone around him and said, "Hey, we need a person to be the goalie. He needs to be someone that's quick and won't allow any balls to get by him. The goalie is the only one on the field who can use his hands. He can catch the ball, knock it away with his hands or head or kick it with his feet. He does whatever it takes to keep it from going into the goal." No one said anything. After what seemed like a long time, Tim raised his hand and said, "Coach, I'll give it a try."

He was thinking about practice when the coach had told them that everyone needed to be a good team player. The team needed a goalie so he would give it a try to help the team. The coach handed Tim special gloves and a brightly colored green shirt so that his teammates would be able to see him in front of the goal. It was time for the game to begin. The coach positioned everyone on the field and Tim in goal.

The whistle blew to start the game. Tim's team all ran to the ball. Ben got to the ball first and kicked it toward the opponent's goal. Duff got the ball and passed it back to Ben. Ben kicked. He scored!!

After the goal, the referee brought the ball back to the middle of the field. The whistle blew to start the game again. This time, the other team got the ball first. They kicked the ball around, keeping it away from the Revolution. It was coming toward Tim. Tim thought, "I can't let them score. I need to be quick and not let any balls in." The ball came closer and Tim got ready. He bent his knees and got his hands out in front of him ready to catch the ball. They kicked it hard at the goal. Tim had to jump up high to catch the ball so it would not go in.

He threw it back into the field to Ben to take it down to the other end of the field. Before the Revolution could score, the other team got the ball back again. They came toward Tim again. This time, they kicked it off toward the side, hoping to get it past Tim. Tim dove to his left knocking the ball out of the way. Ben ran to the ball and kicked it over to Duff. Duff ran down the field kicking the ball ahead of him. He kicked it at the goal and scored!!

The rest of the game was a blur of excitement and Tim's team won 3 – 0. Tim was excited! He had saved 5 balls from going into the goal. Tim and his team celebrated after the game and talked over every goal they had made and every save of the game.

When it was finally time to leave, Tim found Mom and Dad, gathered his equipment and hopped in the car with Christie.

Tim said, "I guess I'm a goalie! That was awesome! I can't wait to tell Chris about the game."

Mom said to Tim, "What's that under your arm Tim?" Tim said, "It's a football helmet, Mom! The football coach asked me to try kicking the football. He wants me to be the kicker on the football team!"

CPSIA information can be obtained
at www.ICGtesting.com
Printed in the USA
LVIW011157230412
278761LV00001B